Christmas Presents
For Him, For Her

A Funny, Festive Cathy & Chris Novella

MARK DAYDY

CONTENTS

1. CATHY

'No, I've never thought of buying Chris a smart suit,' said Cathy, removing her yellow plastic cleaning gloves. 'He's more a striped rugby shirt and Bermuda shorts man – the bolder, the better, so even in a cave you still have to wear sunglasses to look at him.'

'Just trying to help,' said Jasmine, 'as requested.'

'I know,' said Cathy, putting the gloves, can of Pledge and polishing cloth on the coffee table. She'd only mentioned it in passing the day before. Nothing more than an "I wonder what to get Chris for Christmas – any ideas?" Jasmine had seized on it like Indiana Jones finding a clue to the whereabouts of the Holy Grail.

'To be honest, Jasmine, we've got a few days. We'll probably just come up with something at the last minute.'

It was Friday evening and their well-meaning neighbour was overlooking the fact that Cathy and husband Chris had only moved to small town Castle Hill from Finchley, north London on the

Wednesday. Couldn't she see they were still busy cleaning up a grotty house?

'Ooh, how about an ivory cable-knit Aran sweater?' said Jasmine. 'Very rugged.'

'He's already got one – not that he ever wears it,' said Cathy. 'He reckons it makes him look like a folk singer pining for the Orkneys.'

Cathy wondered – how old was Jasmine? Two or three years younger than her? Say, thirty? Certainly old enough to know when the game had ended.

'Would he like to learn the violin?' said Jasmine.

'I hope not,' said Cathy, keen to avoid four years of screeching Mozart-based torture.

She placed a wedding photo of her and Chris on the mantelpiece, then, alongside it, a small brass carriage clock and some "Good Luck in Your New Home" cards. Finally, she added a white porcelain candlestick holder, which she turned to hide the worst of the repairs.

'How about an eternity ring?' said Jasmine.

'He doesn't wear jewellery.'

'Really?'

Cathy looked around the room. Her life was still all cardboard boxes and black plastic bags. It seemed impossible that over half their stuff was in storage in London as they were only due to be in Castle Hill for a year.

'Cathy, I've got it – paragliding lessons.'

'I can't have Chris crashing through someone's loft. He's six foot and thirteen stone; he could do a lot of damage.'

'Hmmm, for a man, he's certainly proving a

challenge.'

Cathy picked up her cleaning cloth. Was Jasmine's life really just an endless round of yoga, Pilates and gift-buying advice?

'When it comes to Christmas presents,' said Jasmine, 'it's the inner person you need to tap into. That's the way to really show each other how much you care. I once worked with a woman who bought her husband an expensive aftershave for Christmas without knowing if it was one he liked. Three years later, they divorced.'

'Yes, well, Chris and I have a very strong personal understanding. We're practically psychic.'

'I'm just saying…'

'I'm serious, Jasmine. Last Christmas we bought each other identical presents.'

Cathy omitted to mention it was gift vouchers.

'Well, if you need any more advice about prezzie-buying, just yell.'

'Thanks, I will.'

'Yes, so – you still haven't said if you want the tree.'

Cathy eyed the tree Jasmine had dumped on the floor. It was a folded-up plastic monstrosity that had seen better days – possibly around the mid-1970s.

'I'm not sure.'

'Only, it's yours to keep and I wouldn't dream of taking a penny for it.'

A penny? That much?

'Just leave it there then. I'll see about putting it in the…' *dustbin, skip, river…* 'bay window. Unless, Chris comes home with a real one.'

That was unlikely. Chris had only popped out for fish and chips. Although, you never quite knew with Chris. He once popped out for a newspaper and came back with a shed.

'Ooh,' yelped Jasmine. 'Poor Roland. I'd better dash in case he's frozen to the spot. Let's have lunch tomorrow. My treat!'

And with that she was gone.

Cathy went to pull the curtains in the drab, un-Christmassy bay window and watched Jasmine totter down the path. Roland, her perfect husband, was outside wearing a snappy dark coat over a suit, waiting to walk her to a restaurant in the town square. And there was Chris, in a brown, pink and blue rugby shirt and green jogging bottoms, his cheeks red with cold, his dark hair nicely unfussy, strolling up to them eating bloody chips from the bag, the swine. He offered Roland a chip but their neighbour treated it like deep-fried plutonium. Undeterred, Chris proffered the open bag towards Jasmine who, in fairness to her, took a couple.

Cathy smiled and pulled the curtains. Jasmine wasn't all bad. She just needed a hobby to fill up her spare hours. But at a loose end or not, was she right about fussing over Christmas presents? Just because someone went on for ages about something didn't make them wrong. That said, Cathy wasn't thinking of buying her man stuff he didn't like. She was thinking of getting him a gift voucher again so he could please himself. But just how personal was that? And did it matter?

She heard Chris at the front door. Could getting

each other gift vouchers two years running really be a warning sign regarding the state of their relationship?

'I want a word with you,' she said as Chris entered the lounge eating.

'I un-un-a-oo.'

'You've only had a few?' said Cathy. 'I'm not talking about chips.'

Chris swallowed. 'If this is about me speeding up the unpacking…'

Cathy threw a bag of assorted towels at him. Then she went over to him, feigned a kiss and grabbed a couple of chips.

'Ha, you fell for it, loser.'

'Not really,' said Chris. 'These are yours. I haven't opened mine yet.'

Cathy chased him into the kitchen, where he stopped, turned and allowed her to run into him. This time they kissed.

'Hang on,' said Cathy, 'I can hear something.'

Meowing.

And the sound of a small furry creature rocketing down the stairs.

Truly-Trudy appeared like the best pet anyone's ever had in the history of the world.

'Who's been sleeping on my bed?' said Chris in a panto kind of way.

Okay, their cat's actual name was Trudy. Cathy named the black and white fur-ball thus when she brought her home from an animal rescue centre. When she called Chris to tell him, he was hands-free on the motorway with a bad signal. Being considerate, he thought why not buy their new family member something personal on the way home. So, he had Truly engraved on a silver identity disc. Well, it cost twenty quid and he couldn't return it, so, the next day, Cathy had the correct name engraved on the other side of the disc. Perhaps that explained their cat's split personality, switching between Olympic super moggy that could do a hundred metres in under ten seconds (at feeding time) to a poor physically incapable feline who simply couldn't budge off Chris's comfy armchair or the bed (at all other times).

At the table, they enjoyed eating their meal off the chip paper and drinking pinot grigio from non-matching glass tumblers. Below them, Truly-Trudy got to work on a mashed cod and cat food combo.

'So, you wanted a word,' said Chris.

'Ah yes. It's just that Jasmine was going on about Roland's prowess in that most vital aspect of a relationship…'

'Choosing the wine?'

'Buying Christmas presents for each other, nitwit.'

'Oh that. What's she been saying?'

'That they get it absolutely right.'

'So do we, gorgeous.'

'I'm serious, Chris Last year, he got Jasmine a weekend spa pass at some top place on the south coast – *and* it was all tailored to her aromatherapy passion with a bit of exfoliation thrown in.'

'Not as exciting as that bobble hat I got you last year. No, hang on, that was the year before…'

'Just shush a minute. It turns out Roland's very creative in the kitchen so Jasmine got him lessons with a top chef.'

'Right, so they're doing about a grand on presents. Seems a bit excessive.'

'The money isn't the point, Chris.'

'Isn't it? Hang on, let me have a quick chat with my wallet and get back to you.'

'Jasmine gives the impression that Roland's able to connect with her soul.'

'He must have bloody good wi-fi then. I have trouble connecting with Yahoo.'

'Chris, this is a chance to reboot what we give to each other.'

'I don't understand.'

'I mean I think we should consider connecting in a strong, personal way.'

'I'll have to let these chips digest first.'

'Stop being silly and listen for once. I'm thinking she might be right.'

'About what?'

'About Christmas presents. I'm not talking about spending big, I'm just asking you to get on board with the idea of buying each other something specially chosen. I can't go through the holidays with the neighbours going on about their trip to the Moon while I'm using a gift token to buy the Best of the Bee Gees.'

'Hang on, let me just run that by my brain. You're saying we should buy each other special gifts... so we can show off to the neighbours?'

'No, Chris, we're...' But Chris was right. Buying

special gifts was a great idea, but not if it was for the wrong reason. 'Forget it. You're right. We don't have time for it.'

'Too right. I'm not buying you something just so you can impress Jazz-whine and Robo-clown.'

'Jasmine and Roland.'

'Just a joke, love. Like they probably call us Crappy and Crud.'

After their meal, they hit the sofa, where Cathy cuddled up to her man – partly because she loved him and partly because the central heating switch was on the blink and the two electric heaters they were using were useless. Truly-Trudy wasn't slow in joining them.

'Do you really think we should think beyond gift vouchers?' said Chris.

'I do, but it's okay if you don't.'

'Do you think it's like some kind of rut? Like we're on the edge of it, in danger of falling in?'

'Could be.'

'We're alright though, aren't we?'

'Of course we are. It's just…'

'Just…?'

'It wouldn't hurt to get each other something better than last year. You know, to show each other how much we care through the power of gift-buying.'

'Stick an extra tenner on the gift vouchers, you mean?'

She dug her elbow into his side.

'Owww,' he exaggerated.

'I mean us getting out there and finding the absolute, ultimate, hundred percent perfect gift.'

'We live in the middle of nowhere, Cath.'

'It's not the middle of nowhere. There are shops and… well, couldn't you use your imagination?'

'You mean it, don't you.'

'I do.'

'You want me to turn hunter-gatherer and find you the perfect Christmas present.'

'And I'll do the same for you. I mean, seriously, how hard can it be?'

'Quite hard, I'd imagine.'

'No way. It'll be easier than you think.'

Cathy snuggled into her man and thought about what he'd love to unwrap on Christmas morning – apart from her, of course. Out there, somewhere, the perfect gift was waiting to be bought. The question was – could she find it?

2. CHRIS

For Chris, Saturday morning was traditionally a time to unwind, to relax, to take stock. A man had to spend time surveying the kingdom of his life otherwise he'd miss bits of it and that would never do. The best way to achieve this state of observation and appreciation, he found, was to establish a base camp in front of the telly and consume a steady supply of hot tea and thickly-buttered toast.

No such luck today though. He was clearing the lounge of its remaining clutter and generally tidying it into a "finished" room.

Cathy wanted a few Christmas touches, so he hung tinsel around a couple of pictures, blu-tacked the Christmas cards they'd received to the wall, and placed a small festive reindeer next to the candlestick holder on the mantelpiece.

He smiled. That candlestick holder had caused him a few problems in the past. He accidentally broke it when they moved into their flat in Finchley. Mild-mannered Cathy blew a fuse and put a thousand-year-curse on him. Well, what idiot leaves a porcelain candlestick holder on the sofa then bloody-well sits on it? She'd bought it at an antiques market as a gift for her unwell gran, but the poor old thing passed away before it could be handed over. Since then, it had become Cathy's memento for a much-missed grandparent and a reminder of the need to act and not dawdle because "we never know what's around the corner".

Chris grabbed his *Fishing Monthly* – freshly caught at the newsagent's earlier – opened it to where he'd left off and switched the telly on. He'd earned a break.

'Oh no, man's worst nightmare…' The remote wouldn't change channels.

It wasn't the remote, of course. He'd only just put new batteries in. It was their landlord's crappy old satellite box playing up, as it had been doing on and off since they moved in.

Chris calmly put his magazine on the coffee table and got to work. While he turned the box on and off, unplugged and re-plugged it, and starting thumping it, Cathy shouted from upstairs not to destroy any of the landlord's property.

'I'm not destroying anything. I'm making improvements!'

It wasn't lost on him that Cathy was in a mood. His assumption that the whole specially-chosen prezzie-buying thing would be a passing phase and that she'd forget the whole thing after a romantic roll around the bed with her loving man turned out to be incorrect. His mistake had been to say so just before the rolling around bit, which turned instantaneously into a non-rolling around bit.

Cathy was upstairs getting ready for a lunch date with Jasmine. Chris was aware that if she mentioned to Jasmine about wanting to adopt a supercharged personalised present-buying approach but that darling hubby wasn't fully behind the idea, Jasmine would reinforce Cathy's resolve with some pseudo-scientific Californian cobblers about relationships. Cathy might leave the house in a "we probably ought to change" mood but she would sure as hell return in full-on "either we change or you can sleep in the shed" mode.

A damp-haired Cathy came down half-dressed and started ferreting through a black bin bag for something. Chris thought she looked so wonderfully natural without any makeup. Of course, once she applied a bit of lippy and did her hair, she'd look more ready to go out, but never more attractive in his eyes.

'Do you really see it as a problem?' he asked.

'Last year, you bought me a gift voucher. The year before, it was a Barnet Football Club bobble hat.'

'That's not what you're looking for in the bag, is it?'

'Chris, we've been buying lazier and lazier Christmas presents.'

'But we love each other and, according to the latest relationship science, that's still quite important.'

Cathy found a black jumper.

'According to Jasmine and Roland, lazy presents

are symptomatic of a lazy relationship.'

'What do they know? I mean it's all show with them.'

'What, showering each other with fantastic gifts they've spent ages thinking about?'

'What's so fantastic about her having her skin scraped off and him peeling onions with a bloke who probably runs a burger van?'

'That is *not* a winning argument.'

'Well, really, I mean what's wrong with a thirty quid gift voucher?'

'I'm just saying we should think about what Jasmine said. I'm not laying down the law, I'm just suggesting we consider buying each other personal presents this year. Have you seen my black leggings?'

'No, but it's like I said – we could always raise our game by raising the amount. Say, forty quid?'

'That's not the point.'

'You can get a lot on Amazon with forty quid.'

'You're not giving it enough thought, Chris.'

'Oh come on, gift vouchers are perfect. They're so damned convenient and you end up with the thing you want. Unless you'd prefer the cash?'

'I'd like you to consider buying me a truly personal present. Something you've thought about. It's just a matter of using your brain. Think, plan, strategize…'

For a man like Chris this wasn't enough information. Men had to have more details.

'Okay, let's take this a step at a time,' he said. 'You'd like me to buy you the ideal gift. One that absolutely nails what you'd love to receive.'

'We've been together seven years – married for five. It wouldn't be all that difficult.'

'Okay, so if I go along with Jasmine's masterplan, what kind of perfect gift would you like?'

'You can't ask me.'

'Why not?'

'What sort of a Christmas present would that be?'

'At least give me a clue then.'

'No.'

'Right. So, you'd be well-chuffed if I went out and got you something you'd absolutely love… which, at this stage, is going to be a big surprise to me, too, because I have no bloody idea what to get you.'

'It's called the thrill of the chase, Chris.'

'Okay, just one question.'

'Which is?'

'What would you get me?'

'Something perfect for you, obviously.'

'Yeah? You do realise the purple shirt you got me two years ago makes me look like a six-foot aubergine.'

'Trust me, I know exactly what to get you. You just have to concentrate on what to get me.'

'Right, so you'd like us to go for it?'

'I would.'

'Well… I suppose that means we'll actually go for it then.'

'Good. You won't regret it.'

'Right then.'

'Right then. Now help me find my leggings

before I freeze to death.'

Ten minutes later, as Cathy met Jasmine on the pavement outside, Chris clapped his hands together in a business-like manner.

'Okay, Truly, let's get to work'

Truly-Trudy, half asleep on the sofa, failed to react, so Chris paced up and down on his own.

'Okay, cat-lifeform, this is the situation. Presents symbolise the state of a relationship and gift tokens say you can't be bothered. No, don't interrupt…'

Truly-Trudy did as she was told.

'…I'm merely stating that side of the argument. I'm not necessarily agreeing with it. However, in order to move on, and get some sanity back into our lives, let's just say the simple elegance of the gift token is a complete non-starter this year. So…'

This created turbulence in Chris's mind.

'What does she like? What does Cathy actually like? What does, Cathy, the love of my life, the sun in my sky, *actually* like?'

He had no idea.

'No – wait! Perfume. Of course. Ha-ha, women are so wonderfully easy to buy presents for. One big bottle of something smelly coming up!'

He went upstairs and checked the shoebox that currently housed Cathy's perfume range. There were seven bottles, all in different shapes and sizes. One or two of them she'd bought herself; the rest were presents. How did you tell which was which? Her mum would have bought one, of course. He'd know that one from its aroma – it would smell like toilet freshener. That woman loved toilet freshener. She sprayed it everywhere, the toilet, the lounge, the kitchen, her armpits. Her favourite was called Caribbean Dream, which boasted a picture of an azure sea and white sands on the bottle. Seriously, what the hell did a beach in the West Indies have to do with a bog in Britain?

But something more than buying the perfume was bothering him. The fact he loved Cathy more than anything in the world would be hard to show if he merely increased her collection of perfume bottles from seven to eight.

Hardly the ultimate present.

So what else did she like?

Fitness stuff?

He looked around their cluttered bedroom. By the wardrobe sat Cathy's neat little case of weight-training dumb-bells. In truth, the only exercise she'd had from them in the past year was carrying them off the removal van and placing them there by the wardrobe.

In fact, the one time she went to the gym, three years ago now, she came back saying, "thirty is the new twenty? No, thirty is the new seventy. I'm knackered."

What else? What else..?

What about buying her seven scarves, each one a different colour. Mauve for Monday, Taupe for Tuesday, white for Wednesday… actually, what colour was taupe? He'd heard of it, but…

No, seven scarves was a terrible idea.

What about a new coat?

Possibly. After all, over the past couple of years, Cathy's two main coats had both mysteriously shrunk. Or at least, that was the only possible explanation for them being too tight. Although, wasn't there talk of a New Year diet and detox?

No, he needed something that wouldn't cause trouble. Something like…

There. On the chair. Black with a strap.

'Handbags!'

And with that, he had solved the dilemma.

A moment later, he was downstairs on his laptop staring at a page full of the things.

He clicked on a yellow one.

Easy-peasy.

3. CATHY

Cathy and Jasmine were studying the menu in *La Cucina*, a small Italian café-restaurant on the High Street. Cathy liked the place. The food looked interesting, the ambience was friendly and it wasn't far to stagger home.

'I meant to say – Chris and I have taken on board your advice.'

'Fantastic. The lounge will look much brighter in warm peach.'

'No, I meant your advice about trying to find the perfect Christmas present for each other. We've agreed to delve into each other's souls, kind of thing.'

'Oh, that's fantastic. Good for you.'

'It's going to be a hands-on experience. We're going to get out there and rummage.'

'Bravo.'

Cathy peered out of the window. Through a gap between the White Horse pub and the Foxglove Tea Rooms, she could see the substantial remains of De Gaul castle, the town's Norman stronghold a quarter of a mile away up the hill. Soaking up the low winter sun, it looked inviting. Of course, Cathy's life would soon be intertwining with the old ruin…

'Let's hope he's not on Amazon,' said Jasmine.

'No way.' *I'll bloody kill him if he is!* 'He wouldn't dream it of it.'

'I was joking, Cathy. Goodness, you really do need to unwind, don't you.' She turned to the waiter. 'Prosecco, please. We have a stressed shopper-to-be.'

Cathy smiled. Maybe Jasmine was right. Maybe the brief settling-in period had unsettled her. Maybe she needed longer to relocate, not just physically, but mentally. They were a long way from their old lives now and the holiday-like mood had vanished leaving her feeling a little lost.

'Thanks for bringing me here,' she said. 'You're right. I do need to calm down a bit.'

The waiter rushed over, popped the cork and poured the wine. They both took a sip.

'Now then,' said Jasmine, 'while Chris is pacing the floorboards working out what to buy you, what have you come up with for him?'

'I haven't given it much thought yet, but it's nothing a couple of glasses of Prosecco can't put right.'

She waited for Jasmine to produce a list of fifty things Chris might like, but it never came.

'Shall we order?' said Jasmine.

Cathy turned her attention to the menu.

'I might try the red mullet.'

'Good choice. It leaves plenty of room for the

lemon cheesecake.'

'Isn't that a bit fattening?'

'It's Sicilian lemon, Cathy – practically part of the Mediterranean diet.'

Once they had ordered, Cathy's mind wandered back to the question of presents. Hopefully, choosing the ideal gift for Chris would be a piece of cake and there would be no need to dwell on it for ages. Maybe she'd deal with it after lunch. That would show him. His perfect prezzie, all wrapped up and placed under Jasmine's old Christmas tree in the bay window in time for *Dr Who* (assuming Chris had got the stupid satellite box working).

She took another sip of wine.

'I suppose it's just a matter of going through all the things Chris would love and choosing one of them.'

Jasmine frowned. 'It takes more than that, Cathy. You need to see into his head, his heart…'

'His soul, I know.'

'That's why I can't help you. Not now you've taken it to the next level.'

'Oh, I see.'

'Obviously, I'll try. That's what neighbours are for. What does he like generally?'

'He likes sport.'

'Playing?'

'Watching it on telly.'

'A season ticket for a football team up here?'

'No, he loves Barnet. I mean I could try to get him interested in a team up here but that's hardly the perfect present.'

'Indeed not.'

'He quite likes rugby… on telly. Maybe I should buy him a telly.'

They fell silent for a moment.

'Go on then,' said Jasmine. 'What's the real reason for moving up here? No-one leaves London for Castle Hill.'

'No, well… it's like I told you. It's mainly work, but more my work-life balance. Basically I didn't have one.'

'It's a big step though, leaving London. Roland and I left Barcelona and it was such a wrench.'

'And you're asking why I left London?'

'My parents lived here. Dad died three years ago, Mum last year. They left me the house and I had this sudden urge to try it.'

'And Roland didn't mind?'

'Oh Cathy, really. You *are* funny.'

'Oh, right.' Obviously Roland wasn't one to argue. At least not with Jasmine.

'Anyway, you're teasing me. You decided to come to Castle Hill and Chris followed you. It's how the world is meant to work.'

'Well, Chris is slightly different. He said he'd give it a year and if it was crap, we'd be high-tailing it back to London.'

'I see.'

'That's why we let out our flat for twelve months and rented a house up here. Less of a bother if we decide not to stay.'

'Well, twelve months is a long time in Castle Hill. They say it gets into the soul, although I haven't quite decided if it's got into mine. That said, you and I could become great friends then neither of us would want to leave.'

'Yes, well, the first part is almost over – the settling in. We've had our few days off to sort ourselves out. From Monday, Chris is back on his laptop doing website content and I start work sorting out your castle.'

'*Our* castle.'

'Our castle, yes.'

Cathy took a swig of wine. She was looking forward to her special secondment as a site manager for British Heritage. Well, why not? She'd been working like mad in London for a decade. Now she was going to enjoy the quiet life at De Gaul castle. Maybe it would only be for twelve months. Maybe it would be for longer. She quite liked not knowing.

'Cathy, you said the other day you were planning to write about it.'

'Yes, I want to dig a little deeper about Guy de Gaul.'

'There's a good booklet on sale in the castle gift shop.'

'Yes, but I have a feeling that's only half the story. Do you ever watch *Who Do You Think You Are?* on TV?'

'I love that show! Oh God, you're not going to tell me Guy de Gaul is your twenty times great-grandfather?'

'I don't know about that. What I do know is my one times grandfather insists we're linked to the castle in some way. Perhaps my twenty times great grandmother boiled the turnips there. Or it could all be nonsense. I'd like to do a little detective work though.'

'It sounds exciting. If you need a sidekick, just let me know. Dad was on the parish council, so who knows what old records we might be able to sneak a look at.'

'Thanks, but don't get too excited just yet. Chris and I need to settle in properly and get through Christmas. But come the New Year…'

'That's the way to see in a new year – with a whole new adventure. I like it.'

They finished off their glasses and Jasmine did the refilling duties.

'So, how long have you and Chris been together?'

'Seven years. Seven happy years. Married for five.'

'But no children?'

'No.'

'Sensible.'

Not for Cathy. She just couldn't have them. Not that she'd share that just yet. If at all.

'I love children, Jasmine, but it's not the right time.' *For my body to do as it's told.*

'Rols and I feel exactly the same way.'

Rols? Ham or cheese?

'Getting back to Chris's perfect Christmas present,' said Cathy, 'Chris loves fishing.'

'Fishing? That's a new one on me.'

'Right, so I'm guessing Roland isn't into it.'

'No, although he's a wiz in the kitchen with a halibut. Does Chris cook?'

'Yes, he's a whiz in the kitchen too.' *Or more like a whirlwind.* 'He does a mean *chilli con carne*. Obviously, you need three pints of ice cold lager to get through it.'

'Oh, Roland loves cooking Mexican. His *sopa de piedra* is to die for. Of course, he has to use local pebbles.'

'Oh right…'

'His black chicken is also incredibly yummy. Has Chris ever cooked black chicken?'

Often, but never intentionally.

'It's just the *con carne* he does. Getting back to fishing, though, there has to be something I can get him. I mean there's a river and canal nearby, so he's bound to give it a go sooner rather than later.'

'What about buying him a new rod?'

'No, buying a man a rod without detailed instructions would be like having him buy me a bra by sight alone. Anyway, he has rods and reels and… basically, he has everything. No, make that three of everything. Maybe fishing isn't such a good idea.'

'No, don't give up. What else can you get a fisherman – apart from a Thermos flask?'

'He's got four of those in varying sizes.'

'Thermal underwear?'

'He's got them in blue, white and grey.'

'A do-it-yourself maggot farm?'

Cathy shuddered. Then she chided herself. It was just a matter of thinking outside the box. Whatever that meant.

After a lovely lunch, Cathy arrived back home. Chris

was on the sofa with Truly-Trudy watching football.

'All done,' he said.

'The satellite box? Good.'

'No, your present. I mean, yes, the satellite box is working after I kicked it a couple of times, but…'

'How can you be all done? You haven't been out.'

'Out? What's that got to do with it?'

'How can you have bought me the perfect gift without moving from the sofa? You haven't got a Tardis in the kitchen, have you?'

'A couple of clicks and it's being delivered midweek. I reckon the internet was specifically invented for blokes.'

'Have you gone mental? How is that personal to the nth degree? You clicked a button.'

'It's a good present.'

'Chris! I demand you cancel the order. I don't care how good it is, it's not what I want.'

'You haven't seen it yet.'

'Right…'

She grabbed his laptop.

'Hey, don't look.'

Following her to the kitchen, he found her with the laptop at the table.

'History, history… Oh, look where Chris has been.'

'Cathy, you are in danger of ruining a perfectly good surprise.'

'Is it a handbag?'

'Cathy, you have ruined a perfectly good surprise.'

'Which one?'

Chris sighed and got the page up.

'There.'

'No, no, no, Chris. No.'

'Are you saying you don't like handbags?'

'What are you on about? I *love* handbags.'

'Then what's the problem? That on the screen there is a handbag. A nice one. Right up your street.'

'Yes, but did you check the quality, the weight, the way it hangs from the shoulder?'

'No, but… it's yellow.'

'Chris, choosing a handbag is like choosing a husband. One mistake and you're stuck with it for bloody ages.'

'Now you're being silly.'

Cathy gave him a look. And a little growl.

'Okay, okay,' he huffed. 'I'll go out! Look, here I am looking for my shoes. See how much I care? I don't even mind that it's cold outside and there's a perfectly good game of football on the telly. Perfectly, poised it is. Two-all with twenty minutes to go. Fancy watching it together?'

'Christopher!'

'I'm going, I'm going… have you seen my shoes?'

4. CHRIS

Chris thought the world of Cathy. And knowing her so well, it was obvious there would be no rest until he'd thrown his weight behind Operation Perfect Gift. The sooner he got her something his hands had been in direct contact with prior to purchase, the sooner they could get back to normal.

Reaching the High Street, he considered his range of options.

Limited.

In fact, he didn't seem to have any.

Looking around, he sought inspiration.

There wasn't any about.

'Come on, Castle Hill, help me out here.'

He found himself staring at a pub. The White Horse, to be exact. It looked like the kind of pub that existed solely to help men faced with the enormity of what they had agreed to do in order to have a quiet life.

'Be strong…'

In a gap between the pub and the Foxglove Tea Rooms, the town's Norman castle looked down on him, all dark and foreboding, or as Cathy preferred – a first class example of Norman workmanship.

'You a tourist?'

Chris turned to find a little old lady wearing a heavy woollen coat and tartan scarf. He guessed she had to be eighty, although guessing people's ages had never been his strongest point.

'I'm a local,' he said. 'A new local.'

'Hang on, you're not the one who's just moved in to Castle Close?'

'That's right. Chris Chappell. I don't think we've met, er…?'

'Grace Darling.'

'That's a friendly manner you've got there, Grace.'

'Darling's my surname. If I wanted to chat you up, I'd flutter my eyelashes.'

'Is she bothering you?'

It was another woman, this time one around Chris's age. One he recognised.

'Me and Grace were just having a chat. I'm Chris, by the way.'

'Kay. I live in the Close just up from you.'

'Yes, I've seen you.'

She was quite a physical woman, what with the chest and wild brown hair. Quite attractive, in fact, which reminded Chris to mention Cathy in any conversations with her.

'Kay's my twin sister,' said Grace, fluttering her eyelashes.

'Now, now, Grace,' said Kay, 'let's not fight over men again.'

'Er, I *am* in a relationship. Just so you ladies know.'

'All men say that,' said Grace.

'Ignore her,' said Kay. 'She's a little man-eater when she's got her false teeth in.'

'He was admiring the castle,' Grace informed Kay, 'unaware of the curse that befalls those who gaze upon it.'

'Is there a curse?' said Chris.

'Might be,' said Grace. 'People believe all sorts of rubbish.'

'Well, I'm a little more scientific in my outlook,' said Chris.

'Is that right your wife is going to be working there?' said Kay.

'Yes, she's with British Heritage. She won't be standing at the door though – you know, boring everyone with what Guy de Wotsit got up to in the dim and distant.'

'No, that's my job,' said Kay. 'Come on, Grace, let's get you home before anything freezes and falls off.'

Chris felt six inches tall.

'I didn't mean that in a negative way,' he called after them somewhat lamely.

He looked up to the castle again. Maybe Grace was right. Maybe there was a curse on all those who gazed on it. Things hadn't exactly got off to a flyer. He didn't even want to live in Castle Hill. Still, he'd agreed to give it a try and a lack of effort on his part wasn't likely to make things better. He'd had his chance to say no. He'd said maybe and Cathy seized on it. But he didn't want to live in London while she was up here for twelve months. It wasn't forever. Just fifty-two weeks. And he was halfway to ticking one of them off. No, he had to make a go of it. And what better way to start than sort out the Christmas present problem.

Of course, he wished he could match Roland's spending on Jasmine. It had to be great to splash out hundreds of pounds without blinking. While Chris's website business could earn a thousand pounds in a week, as it had done during the first week of April, it could also bring in a big fat zero, as it had done during a dozen weeks since that first week in April. The plus point was that he wasn't tied to London. He could earn rubbish money anywhere, even in Castle Hill. And he'd be back at it come Monday, so it was best to get the gift thingy sorted out pronto.

Kay and Grace had stopped a few shops along and were pointing at something in the window. He didn't want them knowing his business so he slipped into the corner shop a la James Bond sneaking into the bad guy's HQ. He was like a shadow, a ghost, a wisp. Chris the Wisp.

Now then, he thought. Chocs or perfume? Or he could get both and still have change out of a twenty. That would leave him enough to get her a Bee Gees CD and a cookery book.

Then he noticed they sold jewellery. Who would have thought it? The local corner shop selling provisions, booze *and* jewellery. No wonder they called them convenience stores.

He studied some earrings. They looked great. He

took them off the rack and held them up to the light.

'Is this real gold?'

'What, at £2.99?'

'Right, so that's what – semi-real?'

'Semi-real? I'm guessing you don't buy much jewellery.'

'Not as such. Or to be more accurate, never.'

'Don't you dare,' said a sinister female voice from the shop doorway.

Chris dropped the earrings onto the counter and picked up a Twix.

'You buy that junk for me and you're divorced.'

Blimey, being stalked by my own wife.

He turned and smiled.

'You've got the wrong end of the stick, Cath. I was merely sizing them up for, er… size.'

'Oh really.'

'Yeah, so I'd have a better picture of the sort of… tat I would be looking to reject when I get to a proper jewellers.'

'Are you buying that?' said the shopkeeper, eyeing the Twix. 'Only people with big hands shouldn't hold chocolate-covered bars. They melt the chocolate. Then I get complaints and there's talk of trading standards…'

Chris handed over some coins.

'Just for the record, Cath, were you following me?'

'Don't be ridiculous. I came out to get you your present.'

'In here? I'm deeply offended.'

'Certainly not in here. A little old lady told me you'd come in.'

'I hope you don't mind me interrupting,' said the shopkeeper, 'but I can see you're new in town. Basically, there's a Castle Hill tradition which states we don't go into people's shops and moan about how terrible it is.'

'I'm sorry about that,' said Chris. 'My wife has been under a lot of pressure.'

Before Cathy could kick him in the ankle, he ushered her outside.

'If we have to go to the nth degree, Cath, let's do it without an argument.'

'That's fine by me. They say it's the thought that counts, so start flipping thinking about getting me the ideal gift.'

'I already am. I'm going into Roxbury. They've got a shopping mall.'

'Chris, you hate malls. They make you tired and irritable.'

'I know, but I love you, Cath, so I'm setting fear and confusion aside and I'm going in there, car park and everything.'

'Oh Chris, please make sure you… you know.'

'Take care?'

'No, have change for the parking machine.'

'Right, well, wish me luck, Cath. If I'm not back by Tuesday send a search party into John Lewis.'

'Oh, if you're going in John Lewis, have a look at their towels. We could do with a new set.'

'Don't confuse me, Cath. I need to stay focused.'

'Yes, okay. Well, good luck.'

Chris hurried back to Castle Close to get their Mini. He'd surely taken on bigger malls than Roxbury. He'd be okay.

5. CATHY

Cathy left Chris to his own devices and wandered further down the High Street. There was a little decorating and DIY shop with an array of power tools in the window. To be fair, Chris wasn't bad at DIY. He knew how to handle a drill and a circular saw. His problem was one of scale. He'd always start a job after breakfast with the words "I'll have this knocked up by lunchtime." The problem was he never specified which lunchtime.

Cathy moved on. There had to be something in town she could get for her husband. He wasn't an alien from Alpha Centauri with exotic tastes. He was Chris from Finchley who liked fishing.

There was a little hobby shop. They had a model railway that ran along the window display and into the shop. It was a brilliant idea for a present. Unfortunately, it was too brilliant. If she bought that for Chris, she'd never be able to set foot in the lounge again. And poor Truly-Trudy would be banished to the garden for fear of a derailment.

As for other hobbies... well, Chris wasn't all that

good at sitting quietly by himself anywhere other than a riverbank. At home, he tended to start by himself, then gradually involve others. Like the time he bought a 1000-piece jungle scene jigsaw puzzle from the charity shop. "I've always loved jigsaws" he pronounced, prior to laying out all the pieces on the lounge coffee table, fitting three bits together incorrectly then, over the next three months, urging Cathy and any visitors to partake of the relaxing benefits of his new hobby.

But he was worth it. While he wasn't God's perfect specimen, she had come to see that she probably couldn't live with Mr Perfect. Too many arguments that he'd win. And Chris had a way of understanding her. Even that first time she'd lain back on the bed, half-naked, waiting for him to rock her world for the first time. When he got alongside her and kissed her on the lips, she thought it best to be assertive and let him know she was up for being kissed in different places. Without a word, he lifted her off the bed, carried her in the bathroom and kissed her there. Then he took her into the spare bedroom and kissed her there. Then, just as she was wondering if he was in fact an idiot, he gave a boyish laugh and said, "It's okay, I know that's not what you meant." After that, to his eternal and ongoing credit, he got it right. *Very* right.

She continued along the street.

A book shop! She loved bookshops. Maybe there was something in there for Chris, too.

Cathy went inside and paused. It was important to soak up the atmosphere of a bookshop. With new books to the left and slightly musty second-hand and collectibles to the right, this particular bookshop was just perfect; a real world of wonder.

'Are you looking for anything in particular?' said a middle-aged woman sorting second-hand books on one of the shelves.

'I do love a good medieval murder mystery, but I wonder if you have anything that might appeal to my husband. He loves football, films... well, what he really loves is fishing, but I can't imagine you'd have...'

'I have *From Barbel to Zander: In Search of an Angling Paradise.*'

'Er...?'

'It's the new one by Jim Rae.'

'Er...?'

'He's a local fishing hero. Bit of a maverick full of homespun advice. You might have seen him on TV?'

'Um...?'

'We do have books on films and football, of course.'

But a thought was forming. A very good thought indeed.

'Did you say he's local?'

'Yes.'

'Exactly how local?'

'Nottbury.'

'Nottbury?'

'It's about three miles up the road.'

Could it really be so easy? She only had to go to Nottbury, track down this local celebrity angler and get him to sign the book. It was simplicity and genius all rolled into one Christmas parcel. Or it very soon would be.

'I'll take it, thanks.'

6. CHRIS

Roxbury Mall was huge. It wasn't built for men, it was built for shoppers. But Chris knew the Yuletide drill. On the last Saturday before Christmas, you had to drive around each of the seven levels until you reached the open bit at the top where the rain was waiting for you. Not that he'd ever been to Roxbury Mall. He just knew.

Five minutes later, getting out of the car and running to avoid a soaking, Chris made a mental note of the level – 7B – then chastised himself for bothering. Unless he suddenly developed the ability to fly, it would be difficult to go any bloody higher.

Reaching the doors to the stairs, he brushed himself off and headed down to the crowded retail levels. At Level 4, he went in through a set of double doors. The cafeteria!

Bloody handy.

No! He was a there on a mission. For some unfathomable reason, the love of his life wanted an ideal gift, and so an ideal gift he would buy her.

After a coffee and a bit of carrot cake.

Fifteen minutes later, Chris was on the concourse studying a map of the mall. Nearby, a choir was singing carols. Chris started singing too. Maybe malls weren't so bad, after all.

'Ho ho ho,' said a voice.

Chris turned to see a vision in… a grey tracksuit holding out half a burger carton containing three copper coins.

'Oh gawd…' He dug out ten pence and placed it in the non-festive receptacle.

Just then, he spotted the shop he wanted. Well, he could hardly miss it. It was enormous and could have clothed and accessorised half the world. Hurrying away from the anti-Santa, he ignored the "20% OFF" signs. They never ever related to anything he wanted and he'd long ago given up bothering.

The first thing he noticed inside was handbags. Loads of them. He checked out a few but they weren't quite right; either too small or too light or the wrong colour. Then, just as he was about to give up, he spotted a beauty. It was stylish, it was classy, it was…

'Nine hundred quid?'

He fled to the next section, where he got squirted with scents.

'I can't…'

'Decide?'

'I can't… b…'

'Believe our latest offers?'

'Brea…'

In danger of becoming the nicest-smelling corpse

in the morgue, he scuttled away to Haberdashery, where the air was clearer. It was an exciting place to be, not because of the reduced-price sewing machines or boxes of stylish buttons, but because of its close proximity to Lingerie.

Sexy lingerie.

Even the red satin stuff with frills.

He moved in, unseen, unnoticed. He was Chris the shadow once more. The ninja shopper.

'Ho ho ho,' said a voice.

'Oh no,' said Chris, turning to see his new friend holding out half a burger carton containing four coins.

'For God's sake, mate. You need to stop seeing me as an income stream.'

'Ho ho ho.'

Chris lobbed another ten pence into the carton.

'Now bog off before I call security.'

'Merry Christmas to you too.'

Chris felt mean, so he flipped a twenty pence piece into the carton.

'Now do me a favour – please don't let me see you again.'

'You've no worries on that score. Not now I'll finally be able to book that flight to Barbados.'

Chris watched him drift away then got back to the business of lingerie. Only there were now two women in their twenties looking at stuff. Well, they were pretending to look at stuff while sneakily watching him. Maybe they thought he was a weirdo. How dare they. He had a mind to go over and explain that he was only there because it was

Christmas. Then his eyes met theirs.

Oh crap.

He smiled in an avuncular fashion.

They giggled.

He left.

By the escalators, he weighed his options.

'Ho ho ho.'

'Oh for fuck's sake!'

Chris escaped the beggar by nipping down to menswear. It was fortuitous too as they had 20% off shoes. He'd been meaning to replace his tan loafers for ages.

'Can I help you, sir?'

'Yes, you see these things on my feet? You haven't got anything similar in size nine, have you?'

'I do believe we have.'

Chris took a seat and let out a sigh. It was good to escape the hurly-burly of shopping, even if he'd only been there twenty minutes and hadn't bought anything. That was the knack with malls. No use charging into it. You had to pace yourself. A shop here, a coffee there, another shop here, half a pint of beer there.

But no, seriously, he was there to buy his gorgeous wife something she'd love. Today, selflessness would be his middle name.

'Now, sir, these tan slip-ons are light but sturdy...'

Ten minutes later, Chris was back on the concourse with a bag containing a pair of light but sturdy tan loafers. Now it was just a case of getting back to the job in hand. The perfect gift for the most wonderful wife on earth. He was always happy when he thought of Cath. Right now it was making him hum a pleasant tune. Or was that because the record shop was playing it?

He loved records shops. They were dying out now, of course, what with downloads. But you couldn't beat having a shufty among the bargain bins. He once bought an Erasure CD for 99p – just because it had a cracked case. Not that he ever played it on the basis that wasn't particularly a fan of the band.

The tune wafting across the airwaves was that classical singer. The opera bloke. The Latin chap with the golden tonsils and lung capacity of a blue whale. Chris hadn't realised he'd recorded a Christmas CD. That would be very Christmassy. Although, seeing it on a little podium on the counter, the sticker told him it was a penny under a tenner. Could he justify that kind of expenditure? After all, he'd just blown forty-nine quid on shoes. No, he had to show restraint. He couldn't waste a tenner on some warbling balladeer – not when they had a New Order compilation on sale *for a fiver!*

An hour later, Chris returned home with his purchases.

'Well?' said Cathy.

'No luck. Sorry.'

Cathy was eyeing his bag.

'Are you sure?'

'Oh, this is just some…' he took the purchases

out of the bag. '…shoes and a CD for me.'

Cathy looked upset about something.

'You alright, Cath?'

'Chris, you failed and you smell like a brothel.'

'Well… maybe I'm not like you and Jasmine. Maybe I can't see inside people's souls like some psychic Peeping Tom. But don't worry. I love you and I will deliver. Tomorrow, most likely. You have my personal guarantee on it.'

7. CATHY

It was Saturday evening, around six, and Cathy was on the phone. Her mum, Denise, had called with all the family news and gossip and was explaining how things were in Finchley.

Cathy huffed. 'Mum, we've only been gone a few days and I knew all that before I left.'

'Well… oh, I bumped into Hayley in Sainsbury's this morning. She's absolutely enormous.'

'Yes, well, she must be nearly there by now.'

Hayley was a neighbour's daughter in her mid-twenties. Her parents had splashed out on a loft conversion so that single mum-to-be Hayley could live there with the baby. Cathy and Hayley weren't exactly mates, what with Cathy being eight years older, but there had been lots of talk about her accompanying Hayley and her baby to the park and the zoo and…

'I also had a Christmas card from Esme, Steve and the girls asking me to pass on best wishes. Nice of them, seeing as you're up there.'

'Yeah, well, they're nice people.'

Esme and Cathy had been on more than a few girls' nights out, although not since Esme had the twins. God, little Izzy and Jem would be two in January. Where did the time go?

'So,' said Denise, 'you're all settled in then.'

'More or less.'

'Truly-Trudy not run off?'

'No chance. The landlord sent a man round earlier to change the central heating switch, so now she has an extensive choice of radiators to curl up by.'

'And Chris is alright, is he?'

'Chris is fine, Mum.'

'Are you sure? If he's there with you and you can't say, just say hotdogs.'

'Don't be ridiculous. Anyway, he's not here.'

'Ah, sneaking back to London, I bet.'

'Don't be daft, Mum.'

'I'm not being daft. Have you checked if the car's still there?'

'The car is…' Cathy peeped through the window '…still there.'

'Well, I won't keep you then. Good luck for Monday. I hope the job is everything you hoped for.'

'I'm sure it will be.'

'Call me in the week with an update. Dad wants to know all the details.'

'I'm sure he does. I'll call you.'

'Okay, take care, Cathy. Love you.'

'Love you too, Mum. And Dad. And Jo. Bye.'

Chris came in just as she ended the call. Cathy

eyed him.

'Not halfway down the M1 then?'

'Eh?'

'Nothing. Now, what are we going to do about dinner?'

There was a knock at the door.

Cathy went to answer it.

'Hi Cathy!'

'Hi Jasmine.'

'How does a nice homemade curry sound?'

'Oh, we couldn't impose…'

'Did somebody mention curry?' said Chris, joining the doorstep party.

'Yes,' said Jasmine. 'I said Roland would knock something up, didn't I?'

'You did indeed,' said Chris.

'You didn't think to share that vital information, Chris?' said Cathy.

'Absolutely, definitely,' said Chris. 'Right up to the moment I forgot.'

'How could you forget that?'

'I was about to drive to Roxbury. I can't be expected to remember Christmas presents and dinner arrangements. Not at the same time.'

'Now listen, Cathy,' said Jasmine. 'This meal is to be enjoyed in your new home. Roland insists. He says it's about establishing a base for conviviality.'

Cathy was flummoxed. 'Um…'

'Now he's cooking enough for six, so are we all systems go?'

'Well, why not.'

'Great,' said Chris. 'And I don't even have to take

my slippers off.'

Jasmine stepped back and signalled down the street with a thumbs up. Cathy was puzzled. Jasmine and Roland lived next door in the other direction.

'Yep,' said Jasmine, 'we have a confirmation from the dynamic duo. You can't do anything in Castle Close without inviting Grace and Kay. Civilization as we know it would crumble.'

'Yes, well…' said Cathy, adjusting to her revised evening. 'It'll be lovely. I've already had a couple of chats with Kay about work, but this is more the right thing. Thanks.'

As Jasmine went off to inform chef Roland, Chris puffed out his cheeks.

'I wished you'd told me about Kay's role at the castle. I made a right mess of things earlier… ah, here they come. Grace, Kay – welcome.'

While Cathy showed Grace into the lounge, Chris held Kay back in the hall.

'Sorry about earlier. I wasn't for a minute suggesting that showing people around the castle…'

'It's fine. It *can* get a bit samey but I do love my summer job.'

'Oh, is it not full-time?'

'No, it's pretty quiet this time of year. I bake cakes over the winter. It's too late for a Christmas cake though. In case you were wondering.'

'Come on, you two,' said Cathy. 'Let's open some wine and get this house-warming started.'

8. CHRIS

Chris used the last of his naan bread to wipe his plate clean. Whatever he'd thought of Roland had been blown away by his homemade bhuna.

'That was fantastic, Roland,' he said, prior to shoving the piece of naan into his mouth.

'Better than a takeaway,' said Cathy.

'Miles better,' said Chris, part-speaking, part-chewing.

'And healthier,' said Roland. 'I'll give you a copy of the recipe, Chris. Jasmine tells me you cook.'

Chris swallowed.

'Well, a bit. Not at this level though.'

'Self-improvement is everything,' said Jasmine.

'Grace knows a thing or two about curry,' said Kay.

'Oh, nothing special,' said Grace. 'I just spent a year in India in the sixties. Anyone remember the Beatles?'

'Greatest band ever,' said Chris. 'Don't tell me you met them?'

'I did.'

Chris was gobsmacked.

'Seriously? You met the greatest band the world has ever known? In India?'

'I did, yes.'

'Really? Did you talk to them?'

'I certainly did. George, mainly.'

'George?' said Jasmine. 'The spiritual heart of the band? What did he say?'

'He said, "give me your hand."'

'Now *that* sounds like the start of a long spiritual journey.'

'No, I'd slipped on a wet patch in the airport terminal and he helped me up.'

'Right…'

'But from then on,' said Chris, 'you and George were firm friends?'

'No, they were all whisked away in a car and I never saw them again.'

'Still, the Beatles,' said Chris. 'I've only ever met Tom Jones. Bumped into him near Oxford Circus. Literally. I was looking the wrong way and bang.'

'People are always bumping into Tom Jones,' said Roland. 'At least, I've heard it's not unusual.'

Everyone groaned at Roland's cheesy joke, but Chris liked that in a man. Telling cheesy jokes was a sure-fire way to warm up a gathering. As long as you stopped at one and didn't think you were on a roll, like that time he had twenty cheesy gags lined up at a friend's wedding party at a posh manor house and, having got a laugh for the first one, ploughed through them to ever diminishing returns. Of course, being lonely at the time and having had several glasses of bubbly didn't help. Still, the gorgeous British Heritage woman who popped in to check that the venue's first-ever party booking was going according to plan meant the evening wasn't a total write-off. Especially when he left early and bumped into her leaving at the same time. Her concern that the venue might be a factor in his early departure led to them talking for ten minutes on a warm summer's evening. When he took her business card, and called her a couple of days later, it wasn't about venue hire.

'I've heard it's temporary,' said Grace. 'Your job, Cathy.'

'It's a secondment; a sort of placement rather than a real job. But, I have plans in place that might change that. We'll have to see how it goes but I might be able to persuade British Heritage to make it permanent. It's all to do with ramping up the tourist numbers.'

'And then what?' said Grace. 'You'd settle?'

'Not sure,' said Chris. 'We haven't planned it down to that level of detail.'

'It's a nice part of the world to bring up children,' said Grace.

'Oh, we…' Cathy began.

'We're not…' said Chris.

As far as he was concerned, this was getting silly. After seven years together, it was time they got their stories straight.

'We're putting it off,' said Cathy.

'Yes.' *Putting off admitting we can't have any.*

'You'll make good parents when you get round to

it,' said Grace.

'So, Grace, how long have you lived here?' asked Chris, very keen to change the subject.

'All my life. I've travelled all over the world but this is home. If I'm away for more than a few weeks, I start to miss it. Don't ask me why. It could be because my family go back a long way and we're tied to the castle. Or it could be something in the water. I'm just a Castle Hill girl. Always have been, always will be. Just like Elsie was, God rest her soul.'

'And what about you, Kay?' said Chris, keen to move on from Elsie, who had died in this very house a year earlier and whose son had left it empty for a grot-gathering age before deciding to rent it out. 'Does the place keep you here?'

'Me? No, I'd be off like a shot if Mr Right came over the hill in his white sports convertible waving plane tickets to California. Or frankly, Mr Okay on roller skates waving train tickets to Cleethorpes.'

'She says that,' said Grace, 'but she won't leave. Not after last time.'

Kay sighed. 'I did live in Manchester for two years. But divorce has a habit of interfering with a good marriage, so I came back. It doesn't have to be forever though.'

As Cathy poured everyone more wine, Chris pondered that notion. Castle Hill didn't have to be forever.

Later, in bed, Chris wondered about the move they had made. Of course he was a hundred percent behind Cathy's new job and all that went with it. But he was already thinking of all the Barnet FC home matches he was going to miss, and particularly the few pints with his mates afterwards. Not that football was as important as Cathy's happiness. His greatest concern was that she might be running away from things. He knew how much she wanted a baby, but Nature had decided she would have a seriously reduced chance.

So, for Chris, a question kept nagging away. Did the fact that a number of Cathy's friends had or were due to have babies influence her decision to take a twelve-month posting a hundred miles away? And were babies popping out of everywhere the real reason she was hoping to make the move permanent? People had babies in Castle Hill too. Okay, so Cathy didn't know the mothers – yet. You couldn't hide away from people though. She would have to smile sweetly at someone's sprog sooner or later.

Of course, Cathy would say her connection to the castle was the reason she had come. And he couldn't argue with that. There was a long-standing family story bordering on a Disney fantasy that her family had once owned the castle. Chris didn't believe it for a second and was convinced this ancient ownership story probably referred to a pub called The Castle.

Either way though – baby or ancient knights of the realm – would he continue to support her if she wanted to make the move permanent? All he had to guide him was his love for her. Fortunately, that was exactly the same size as the Universe so, at the very least, she was guaranteed a fair hearing.

And with love in mind, he gazed into her eyes. Only they were closed.

'Night, night, Cath,' he whispered.

9. CATHY

It was Sunday morning and Cathy and Chris were in bed exchanging views. Cathy knew that Chris would have rather been doing something else in bed with her, but that wasn't the point. She hadn't forgotten his failure at the mall.

'What did you call it?'

'An oversight,' said Chris. 'Obviously, I should have bought you something from the mall, seeing as that's why I went there. I just couldn't find anything that suited you.'

'In a whole mall, you found nothing?'

'Obviously, I couldn't look at everything otherwise I'd never have got out of the place.'

'I can't believe you couldn't think of anything to buy me.'

'It's not my fault you suddenly stopped liking gift vouchers.'

'It's not my fault you're more interested in buying things for yourself.'

'Now you're being silly.'

'Silly? You drag me thousands of miles from

home to live in the middle of nowhere…'

'A hundred, and it was your idea.'

'What's that got to do with it? Can't a woman have a rant without you coming over all factual?'

Chris sighed. 'I think I'll make us some tea. Unless you fancy…?'

'Milk, no sugar, thank you!'

Chris pulled his dressing gown on and slipped out of the room.

Cathy gave it a moment then followed him down to the kitchen. Without a word, he opened his arms and she stepped into his embrace. Truly-Trudy, ever hopeful of being fed or pampered, stretched then climbed out of her basket by the kitchen radiator and began circling their legs.

Chris kissed the top of Cathy's head.

'Wife, I'm going to buy you the best-chosen Christmas present on Earth – even if it kills me.'

She looked up at him. 'Sorry for shouting.'

'It's to be expected. You've cocked up our lives with a daft move and it's only right that someone else should take the blame.'

'Well, I'm glad you can see the logic of it.'

Cathy reached up and kissed him. That's what she loved about Chris. They could have a little spat one minute and it would all be forgotten the next.

'You're a good man, Chris.'

'I know, love.'

'Bone-headed, pea-brained and awkward, but…'

'…cuddly?'

'Yes, cuddly.'

'Does that mean…?'

'No.'

'No?'

'No, you oaf. You have got to go out there and find me the perfect Christmas present.'

'I was just about to make some tea.'

'After a cup of tea then. But this is serious, Chris. You need to get out there and forage. And not any old tat from the corner shop, either. I want something you've bought with love.'

'They only take cash or credit cards in Castle Hill.'

'Use your instincts. Back in caveman days, men were hunter-gatherers. So go out there and hunt and/or gather something.'

'I will, Cath. I'll don a loin cloth and get out there.'

'Good.'

'As soon as I've had my cup of tea, some Oat Flakes and a shave. Um… so what about you? What will you be up to while I'm out there on the windswept gift plains?'

'I've got a plan. A simple one. In fact, I'm already halfway through it. While you're huffing and puffing in a state of confusion, I'll be wrapping up the perfect present for you.'

'You make it sound so simple.'

'It is for a woman. I'd say watch and learn, but I can't give away trade secrets.'

'Right. And you're sure we haven't got time to nip upstairs for a quick…?'

'Oh, alright then, Caveman – but I can only spare half an hour. No, make that an hour.'

*

An hour and a half later, in the car on the way to Nottbury, Cathy wondered how much Chris loved her. Yes, he clearly desired her; that was in absolutely no doubt. But that was lust. She thought back to what he said about her admitting she'd put on two stone since they first met. What were his actual words? She had to remember them correctly. Yes, he said "how about nipping back to bed while it's quiet, you sexy woman, you." Was that love? Or just bad eyesight?

She sighed. He wouldn't really buy her duff earrings and a Twix for Christmas. She was letting too many things get jumbled up and it was too easy to reach a tangled conclusion. Even while he was on top of her going like a well-oiled steam train, he always whispered "mmm, mmm, Cathy, Cathy, Cathy…" Well, if that wasn't enough to take a girl over the edge in a Niagara Falls of ecstasy, what was? And he often told her he loved her, and backed it up with hugs and cups of tea. He even did the washing up occasionally. So, with all that in mind, how come the big pillock couldn't think of the perfect present to buy her?

No, she had to trust him, even though he was only a man. She had to give him the time and space to get his head around the concept. Okay, so his track record wasn't good. The Princess Leia earmuffs of four years ago, to keep her ears warm while cycling. Too bloody thick. That first time she set off wearing them, cycling down the front garden path as he was coming back from the paper shop, she never had a chance of hearing him call over the top of the hedge, "watch out for this Thames Water bloke lifting the manhole cover."

10. CHRIS

Putting his coat on in the hall, Chris pondered his options. If he wanted to go back to the mall, he'd have to get a bus or a train. Did they even have a bus or a train that went there?

But no, he wanted to try something different. Okay, so there wasn't much time left before the Big Day, but he wanted to come over all psychic and see if the fates had anything to say for themselves. Not that he was psychic, or believed in the fates.

Outside, he bumped into a familiar figure.

'Hello Kay. How's things with you?'

'Fine thanks, Chris. Last night was good fun, wasn't it.'

'Yes, it was. I'm glad you and Cathy get on so well. Seeing as you'll be working together come Easter.'

'You've got a lovely wife.'

'Yes, but…'

'But?'

'But I'm not sure what to get her for Christmas.'

'Oh.'

'I need to get her something really nice but I'm at a complete loss.'

'You've left it a bit late, Chris. How about a gift voucher?'

'Kay, really. That's a terrible idea – and exactly what I got her last year. No, this year I thought I'd go for something personal.'

'What a lovely man you are.'

'Yes... well no, it was Cathy's idea. No, make that Jasmine's idea.'

'Ah, right. Well, what does Cathy like?'

'Oh... well... you know... kind of... women's... sort of... thingy. You know.'

'Clothes?'

'No.'

'No? Are you sure?'

'Well, obviously, she likes them, but I want it to be more personal.'

'Perfume?'

'No, it's not quite...'

'What about a handbag?'

'Best not go there.'

'Knick-knacks?'

'Er...'

'Antique knick-knacks? I mean you don't want to clutter the place with rubbish, but a well-chosen piece can work a treat.'

'Antique knick-knacks. Possibly...'

'There's an auction at Taylor's today.'

'Is there?'

'Yes, they're usually pretty good. You occasionally get people coming from afar to have a nose around. Do you know Taylor's?'

'Er, no.'

'End of the High Street. They've got a place behind the shop. It's at lunchtime, I think.'

'Kay, you're a star. Thanks very much.' Chris headed off to the High Street, but called back. 'If I discover a Picasso, I'll cut you in!'

Less than ten minutes later, he was outside Taylor's Antiques shop. A sign pointed down a side road where a few cars had parked up on the grass verge.

Chris ventured down there. At the end, it opened out to reveal a shabby barn-like building. By the door a sign stated: "Auction Preview 10am-12 noon".

The interior was an improvement on the exterior. While it wasn't a state-of-the-art barn conversion, it felt just right for showing off old paintings and antique pottery. Chris grabbed a catalogue, which was in fact a sheet of paper, and started off by trying to expertly study a watercolour of birds flying over a river. Was this a lost classic of British Victorian art? Or a student work from last week? How did you tell?

He moved on to a small brown jug. How much would that fetch? Was its overall juggishness of a calibre to bring a dealer over from New York? Or would it go for two quid because it was rubbish? Was there really a way to tell? Or did the experts just make it up as they went along?

He moved on to the next few items. A small brass clock. Nope. A salt and pepper set. Nope. A china tiger. Nope.

Then…

No…

Surely not…

On display between the tiger and two old fountain pens was a white candlestick holder. Chris felt psychic rumblings.

'Hang on one second…'

He whipped out his phone and feverishly started searching.

The photo… the photo… the photo…

Yes, the photo of Cathy and her sister Jo at the flat in Finchley… the two of them, in front of the mantelpiece… and to one side of them… the candlestick holder…

'Exactly the same! How brilliant is that!'

He studied Lot 12 a little closer. It appeared to be in very good condition…

'Seen anything you like?' asked a jovial old man with a walking stick.

'No,' said Chris, putting the candlestick holder back and stepping away.

He wasn't falling for that old tosh. The walking stick was obviously a prop and the friendly chit-chat a way to disarm competitors.

Annoyingly, the man cast an eye over the candlestick holder. Inwardly, Chris felt like a volcano that was about to blow. Outwardly, he simply shrugged.

'Bloody old tat,' he huffed before moving on to study some dining furniture.

Surely, no one else would be interested in the

candlestick holder. He stole a glance back at the walking stick man. He was checking the base of the bloody thing. Hopefully, he'd see it was a bit of old dross and forget about it.

11. CATHY

Cathy slowed to thirty miles an hour as she entered Nottbury, and then slowed to around ten as she spied two men outside a pub. Reducing her speed to a crawl, she hoped they were local. After all, they looked local. Although… how could anyone look local? But no, why else would they be outside a pub in Nottbury?

She lowered her window and called to them.

'Excuse me, you wouldn't know Jim Rae, would you?'

'Yeah.'

'Oh brilliant. Can you tell me where I can find him?'

'Come and have a drink and we'll tell you all about him.'

Oh gawd. Neanderthals.

She drove on fifty yards, slowed, and called to a woman walking past with a well-behaved spaniel.

'Excuse me, do you know where I might find a man called Jim Rae?'

The woman pondered it for a moment.

'Yes, I think he's on Channel Four.'

'Yes, but…' *God save us from twits…* 'do you know where he lives?'

The woman shrugged then looked around as if hoping Jim Rae might be walking by.

Cathy would have enquired further but an agitated traffic jam was forming behind her. Frustrated, she drove on another hundred yards and found a space to pull into. It was by a cottage where a man was putting some bottles into a recycling box.

'Hello, sorry to bother you,' she said. 'I'm trying to find Jim Rae.'

'Jim Rae?'

'Yes.'

'What, *the* Jim Rae?'

'Yes.' Obviously, this man knew half a dozen lesser Jim Raes.

'You mean Jim Rae the angler?'

'Yes, Jim Rae who's an angler on TV and writes the occasional book. *That* Jim Rae.'

'He's good, he is. Uses old knowledge, not all the modern rubbish you get nowadays.'

'Yes, do you know where he lives?'

'You're in luck. He lives in this village.'

'Er, yes, I gathered that.' *As opposed to trying this village at random.* 'Am I far?'

'Far from where?'

'From Jim's house.'

'No, not far. Less than two hundred yards, I'd say.'

'In what direction?'

'That direction, obviously.' The man chuckled at

the idea it could have been in the opposite direction.

'Okay, let me shorten this,' *before the Sun runs out of gas...* 'If I drive that way for roughly two hundred yards...'

'...and turn left by the white post...'

'...I'll get to Jim's house.'

'No, you'll get to the old phone box. Don't try using it, mind. It don't work.'

He seemed to find that funny too.

'Yes, so, from there...'

'Look around you. You'll see a house.'

'A house?'

'Yes, a house.'

'And that's Jim's house, is it?'

'No, that's Roy Murray's house. But if you go to Roy's and look left...'

'I'll see what exactly?'

'Jim's cottage, obviously. What else would you expect to see?'

The man went inside. He clearly wasn't used to dealing with fools.

Cathy drove off with the directions burned into her brain. Two minutes later, she pulled up by a disused phone box and got out of the car. Without delay, she walked briskly over to Roy Murray's house and looked left.

Bingo.

It was a lovely little cottage with a thatched roof. Had Cathy owned it, she would have been outside with a tin of paint, brightening the place up a bit. She would have also removed the "Keep Out" signs. Two of the little blighters – white background, unfriendly red lettering – spoiled the view.

'Oi!'

Cathy peered up the long path to the front door. There was man in a fishing hat staring at her.

Cathy pointed at a sign.

'Do these apply to everyone?' she asked. 'Only I'm not a fan or anything.' No, hang on, that probably wouldn't make him warm to her. 'I mean I've never read any of your books or seen your TV shows, so who knows, I might be a fan in waiting. Cold day, isn't it.'

'Why are you approaching the house?' he said, looking uneasy about the shrinking distance between them.

'I can see you don't like visitors.' Cathy held up the carrier bag containing the book. 'It's just that my husband's a big fan of yours. Give him some worms and a wet day and he's in heaven. So, shall we do it inside?'

'Do what inside?'

'You sign the book for me. Well, for Chris, actually. I'd be ever so grateful if you could write something like… er… Dear Chris…'

'Piss off.'

'Dear Chris, Piss Off… No, he wouldn't like that. I was thinking more "Best Wishes", kind of thing.'

'I ain't signing no book.'

'Just your name then.'

'Clear off before I call the police.'

'Oh come on, it's only six letters. If you'd been born Cornelius Fotheringbridge Carbuncle, you'd have a case.'

Jim Rae produced a mobile phone, pressed a few buttons and put it to his ear.

'Police? … It's Jim Rae in Nottbury … Yes, another one.'

'Well, look, I can see you're busy, Jim. I'll give you some time to think about it, shall I?'

Cathy retreated back to the car. Now what? She could hardly get herself arrested. You wouldn't get much shopping done from inside a police cell.

But what if the old so-and-so was bluffing? Maybe it was his regular party piece, to pull out the phone and pretend to call the police. She'd wait and see.

Fifteen minutes and no police later, Cathy crept back towards the house. And there he was, putting his fishing stuff into his car. The bloody fibber! She hurried back to her own car. She'd follow him. Hunt him down and… no, just follow him to see where he was going.

A moment later, he drove past. He wouldn't have seen Cathy due to her ducking down and head-butting the gearstick. As soon as he turned onto the main road, she gunned her engine, turned and followed.

A few hundred yards down the road, she felt incredibly alive. It was quite a thrill to follow someone. A few miles later, she wasn't quite so thrilled. Where the hell was he going? What if he was on his way to a fishing competition in Scotland? Exactly how far did the likes of James Bond follow someone before deciding it was a bit too far?

Moving on to whether James Bond ever worried about his work-life balance, she found herself continuing to follow the foul-tempered fisherman off the main road and down a country lane. Wherever he was going, it wasn't Scotland. Very likely, it wouldn't be too far now.

Five minutes later, Cathy's prey pulled into a rough parking area. It was big enough to hold a hundred vehicles, so the five cars there had plenty of space. Even so, they were bunched together like reindeer in fear of a wolfy-teethy-thing leaping out of the bushes.

Cathy held back as Jim Rae pulled up alongside them. He didn't hang around. Grabbing his gear from the car boot, he headed off down a path that disappeared behind the trees.

Pulling into the car park, Cathy ran into an etiquette dilemma. Should she pull up alongside the scared reindeer cars? Or park separately.

She did the latter, feeling it would avoid any sense of her intruding. That said, when she glanced back from the path, her little Mini now looked like a scared-vulnerable-thingy separated from the pack. She half-expected to return to find it upside-down in a pool of oil with its engine ripped out.

As the path reached the trees, it took Cathy down to a big stream. Well, a small river. She wasn't actually sure at which point the former could be called the latter, or if there might be an in-between word.

Continuing along the path, she found the water

running into a bigger, slower-moving river. Here there was a flat bank with lots of places you could sit and fish. Indeed, that's exactly what half a dozen men were doing.

She decided to give Jim Rae time to set up his rod, then she'd happily and coincidentally pass by and see him.

While she waited out of sight, she wondered what men saw in dangling a rod over water in the hope of catching something slimy and wriggly. She preferred her fish in breadcrumbs. Still, she supposed Chris would be in his element here. In fact, she would make a note of the route so he'd have access to what had to be good waters.

A few minutes later, she decided it was time.

Instead of a full-on charge up the path, Cathy opted for a touch of jungle warfare. Yes, she'd sneak through the bushes and appear behind him in a kind of "You're A Celebrity, Get Me Out Of Trouble By Signing Here".

Annoyingly, the bushes were a bloody nuisance – thick and tangled and nothing like the local park back in Finchley. Pushing through them regardless, Cathy made steady progress until she wasn't too far from Jim. In fact, parting the foliage in front of her, she had a perfect view of his unfriendly back. How happy he no doubt was, sitting there in his silly hat with his silly rod like an oversized garden gnome.

It was time for action.

She leapt out and sprang forward.

'Wow, amazing, the lovely Jim Rae!'

'No,' said the man, turning. 'Jim's over there.'

Same bloody hat!

'Sorry.'

Drat. Stripped of the element of surprise, she pasted on a huge grin and danced up to Jim Rae, who was sitting on a canvas stool, ten yards upriver.

'Jim! Fancy bumping into you here!'

'Please go away. You'll frighten the fish.'

'What?' Was that even possible? She hadn't made any direct threats against them and anyway, surely skewering their jaws with hooks was more frightening to the average guppy than the sound of a chatty woman.

Cathy lowered her voice.

'Jim, you'd be doing me a massive favour if you'd sign your book for my husband.'

'I'm busy, please go away.'

'Jim, if you don't sign it, I'll shout very loudly and frighten all the fish away.'

'You do that and I'll have the police onto you.'

'I'm not falling for that again.'

'You don't believe me?'

'Go on, I dare you. Call the police. And if they don't turn up in the next ten minutes, you'll sign this book. Deal?'

'Deal.'

'What, really?'

'Yes, really.'

'Okay… ten minutes then.'

Jim looked over to the man Cathy had leapt out on first.

'Dave? You got a minute?'

Dave came over.

'Everything alright, Jim?'

'Let me introduce you two. This is Detective Inspector Dave Hanley, and you are…?'

'I am… just leaving, Inspector Dave.'

Cathy legged it all the way back to the car, got in, revved up and drove away. The whole thing had been a disaster. There would be no personalised prezzie for Chris.

What a failure…

Half a mile down the road to Castle Hill, she screeched to a halt.

'He's bloody well done it again!'

She turned around and raced back.

'Detective Inspector Dave Hanley, my arse!'

Five minutes later, Cathy pulled up alongside the fishermen's cars.

'Right, this requires a plan.'

She got out and paced up and down. Then she opened the boot.

'Drat.'

She'd been hoping Chris had left his fishing gear in the car, but there was only his old fold-up fishing seat.

Even so…

A moment later, she was heading down the path towards Jim Rae and friends.

'Hi all. Me again.' She planted her fold-up seat between Jim and the fake cop. 'Ah, this is the life. We can have a good old chin-wag. I'm assuming that's not against the law?'

'Please go away,' said Jim.

'I'm not committing an offence, Jim.' She turned to the rogue detective. 'It's Dave, isn't it? This is a public space, is it not? So, I'm okay here, right?'

'Jim doesn't like the public invading his private space,' said Dave. 'And neither do I.'

'All fisher-folk together, eh? Just the right people, then, because I'm planning to join you. Become one of the fraternity, so to speak.' She eyed the pair of wellies alongside Jim's bag. 'Ooh, lovely wellies, Jim. Is that the kind of footwear I need to be authentic?'

To ensure maximum annoyance, she took her shoes off and tried them on.

'Haven't you got small feet, Jim. Hang on...'

Something was worryingly not right.

'You're squashing my maggots,' said Jim.

'What?'

'He keeps them in a bag in a fur-lined welly,' said Dave. 'The warmth makes them more wriggly.'

A loud scream escaped Cathy's throat. She began hopping furiously, desperately trying to pull the maggot-infested welly off, but only succeeded in falling over Chris's fold-up seat and crashing into the water.

'Shit!'

Thankfully, the water was only two foot deep...

And...

Actually...

Falling in didn't need to be a complete disaster. Jim Rae now had a damsel in distress to deal with. What better way to elicit sympathy?

'You couldn't help me, could you?' she asked.

Jim sniffed and ignored her, even though she was

only two yards in front of him and waving her arms.

'Jim?'

'You're scaring the fish,' he said.

Cathy sighed. Then grabbed the end of his rod...

'Hey, let go.'

...and used it to pull herself out...

...and Jim Rae in.

'Aarghhh...' he managed to say before drinking some of the river.

Dave got up. 'If you don't leave right away, I'll have to caution you for a breach of the peace.'

'Not now, Dave. I'm busy with Jim. Are you alright there, Jim? How about we get this book signed, then I can disappear to spread your legend far and wide.'

'I won't ask you again,' said Dave.

'Oh dear. Next you'll be pulling out your little police ID card.'

Dave pulled out his little police ID card. It stated: Detective Inspector David Hanley.

'It's a good picture of you, Dave. Photo-booth or selfie?'

'Is your husband a regular fisherman?' asked Jim, climbing onto the bank.

'Yes. Yes, he is,' said Cathy, turning to him with rising hope.

'I'm bloody-well not surprised!'

Cathy sighed. There was obviously some kind of police angling branch of the freemasons in these parts. It wasn't unreasonable to bet that another of his fishing buddies was a local magistrate. Good grief, she could be starting a five-stretch before she was dry if she wasn't careful.

'Well, I'll um…'

She grabbed her shoes and book and began the slow soggy march back to the car.

'Bloody public,' hissed Jim. 'Why can't they stick to the bookshop signings!'

Bookshop signings?

Bloody hell. So, obtaining a signed copy of this rod-wielding rodent's new book was actually the easiest thing in the world – except for Cathy, who would very likely be chased out of any bookshop containing Jim and hunted down by police with helicopters and sniffer dogs.

12. CHRIS

The auction was due to start in ten minutes. There were a few people milling around outside and Chris smiled politely at anyone who looked his way. He even chatted briefly about the weather with a lady who looked like Mary Poppins. The main thing was to stay cool so that you didn't let the opposition know you were desperate for the candlestick holder. He'd seen that in an old episode of *Lovejoy* on telly.

Inside the barn, the sale items had been moved to make way for about thirty chairs, all facing a small podium from where the auctioneer would no doubt conduct his business.

Chris checked the sheet of paper with the lots listed then went to register his details with the auctioneer. Once he'd signed up, he was given a small paddle with a number 23 on it.

'Did you settle on anything?' asked the jovial old man with the walking stick.

Chris was disappointed to see him. People like that were only ever trouble.

'I never saw anything I liked,' said Chris, matter-of-factly.

'Right, so you've just registered even though you don't intend to buy anything. Understood.'

Chris was determined to get rid of him.

'Actually, there was a nice table,' he said, referring to a drab item he'd seen earlier. 'Victorian.'

'You don't sound local. What is that accent? London?'

'Could be.'

'I see. And is this what you do?'

'Not as such, no.'

'I suppose it all depends, does it?'

'Oh, absolutely.'

Chris tried to remember what the hell they were talking about.

'Victorian then,' said the man.

'Yes, a table.'

'Hmmm. And you reckon…?'

'Mmmm. I do.'

A few minutes later, with around twenty people present, the auctioneer called the room to order.

'Welcome to today's auction, ladies and gentlemen. I can see you're all big spenders so let's get started. First up, we have a late-Victorian milk jug. A lovely piece, perfectly proportioned, delightfully weighted… do I hear ten pounds? Ten pounds anyone? Who's going to start us off?'

Chris felt a weird urge to bid.

No!

He'd read somewhere about something called auction fever. He was on a limited budget and Cathy would kill him if he came home with a perfectly proportioned, delightfully weighted, completely useless milk jug. After all, he didn't actually want it and they had been getting along just fine pouring their milk straight from the plastic bottle.

It sold for eight pounds.

Next up was a blue china plate that went for twenty-five. Then came the Victorian table. Neither Chris nor the man with the walking stick bid for it. It went for sixty-two pounds to the lady who looked like Mary Poppins.

Next came a small Georgian writing desk. Chris liked the look of it. It was exactly the sort of character item he needed for putting his…

What was he doing? He was there for Cathy, not for himself. He studied the sheet. Lot 12.

Concentrate.

Lot five looked good.

No. Lot bloody twelve.

Eventually, it came around.

'A nice white porcelain candlestick holder,' said the auctioneer. 'Lovely condition. Who'll start me at twenty pounds? Twenty? Twenty anyone?'

Chris remained calm, aloof, uninterested.

'Ten then. Anyone wish to bid ten pounds? Come on, ladies and gentlemen, it's in lovely condition.'

Mary Poppins raised a finger.

'Ten pounds, thank you, madam. Do I hear fifteen? Fifteen, anyone? No? I'll take twelve then. Twelve, anyone?'

Chris half-closed his eyes as if he'd prefer to sleep than buy such inconsequential tat.

'Twelve? Anyone? I'm selling at ten then… once… twice…'

Chris opened his eyes. He'd almost nodded off. His hand shot up and waved the paddle.

'Twelve, thank you, sir. Do I hear fifteen?'

Mary Poppins raised a finger.

'Thank you, madam. Twenty anyone?'

Chris raised his paddle and shot death rays at Ms Poppins.

'Twenty, I'm bid.'

The Poppins finger went up again.

'Twenty-five, thank you, madam.'

Chris wasn't finished. Not by a long chalk. He dispensed with the paddle and nodded surreptitiously.

'Thirty, I'm bid. Do I hear thirty-five? Thirty-five? No? I'll take two. Thirty-two pounds anyone? Going once to the buyer from London temporarily staying in Castle Hill for thirty pounds then… and twice… and thank you, Eric. I have thirty-two. Do I hear thirty-five?'

Eric? Who the hell's Eric?

The man with the walking stick smiled at him.

No, you arse! I haven't come up from London to buy a bloody candlestick holder!

'No? Going once…'

Chris raised a hand.

'I have thirty-five. Do I hear forty?'

Eric raised his stick.

'Thank you, Eric. Do I hear forty-five?'

Chris wasn't happy, but he wasn't letting bloody Eric have the damn candlestick holder.

'I'm selling to Eric at forty then…'

As casually as possible, Chris raised an I-almost-can't-be-bothered two fingers at the auctioneer.

'Forty-two from our London friend. Do I hear forty-five?'

Eric made a gesture.

'Forty-three. Thank you, Eric. Any advance on forty-three?'

Right, time to burn the little swine.

'Forty-five,' said Chris.

'Fifty,' said Eric.

The crowd gave a little "oooh".

Chris was crestfallen. This wasn't an auction, it was an ambush. While he wrestled with possible strategies and budgets, he heard:

'And sold to you, Eric.'

Chris was appalled.

'Next item, a lovely watercolour painting.'

Chris stormed out. He'd have to find some other perfect gift. But how? There was hardly any time left or any place to go.

Eric came out and gave Chris a sympathetic smile. But Chris didn't want his sympathy. He wanted his candlestick holder.

'I'll buy it off you.'

'It's not for sale.'

'Go on, I'll give you forty for it.'

'I just paid fifty.'

'Yes, but as a London antiques specialist I can now reveal it's complete shit and only worth a fiver. Frankly, I'm doing you a favour.'

'I'm not interested.'

'Alright, fifty-one pounds then. A clear one pound profit. Can't say fairer than that, can I.'

'You're forgetting the ten percent the house adds on.'

'Fifty-six then. The auctioneer's fee plus a whole pound on top.'

'No.'

'Fifty-seven?'

'No.'

Eric hurried away. Chris wondered what to do. He'd had a psychic connection with that candlestick holder. It wasn't just because it matched Cathy's; they were very likely made by the same skilled Victorian hands as a pair.

He hurried down to the High Street but Eric had vanished.

'Damn!'

It was a now a fifty-fifty. Left or right?

Chris turned right and got going. Hopefully, he'd soon have Eric in his sights.

'I bet he's bought it as a Christmas present for someone,' Chris grumbled. 'He'll probably tell them it cost him a hundred, the tight-arse.'

There!

He caught up with Eric by the King's Head pub.

'Are you following me?'

'Who me?'

'Yes, you.'

'Look, Eric, I won't beat about the bush. I'm after that candlestick thingy you bought.'

'Of course you are. You came all the way from London for it. Even hired some local accommodation to make sure you didn't miss out. I'm not stupid, you know. Worth a few hundred, is it?'

'A tenner at most, but it'd make a great pair seeing as my wife's already got one.'

'Ah, I get it. Okay, fair enough. Twenty quid.'

'Twenty? You'll let me have it for twenty? Oh that's brilliant.'

'No, I'm offering *you* twenty for your wife's one. Then I'll have a pair. I'm not daft, I watch the *Antiques Roadshow*. If you've got a pair of anything, they're always worth a lot more.'

Chris tried to remain calm. It wasn't easy.

'Look, Eric, try to see this from my point of view.'

'A London wheeler-dealer's point of view, you mean? I'll have you know I wasn't born yesterday.'

'I'm not a wheeler-dealer. I'm just an ordinary bloke. It's supposed to be a Christmas present for my wife, Cathy. She's a lovely woman. Does a lot of work in the community and sends money to kids in Africa.'

'Your wife, Cathy? That's a good one. Do they teach you that in wheeler-dealer school?'

'Eric, she's not just my wife, she's the sun in my sky, my heaven, my soul mate.'

'Well... put like that... alright, it's yours for a hundred quid.'

'A hundred? That's a bit steep!'

'For a soul mate?'

Chris was stumped. He couldn't afford it. And yet, he had to have it.

'Make up your mind, Mr Wheeler-Dealer.'

Chris wracked his brain.

'I'm trying.'

'A hundred and ten,' said Eric.

'What?'

'That's the thing with these sought-after items. The price keeps going up.'

'You'd do well in London, Eric.'

'Do we have a deal then?'

Chris sweated. He needed an instant plan that would make the despicable Eric sell him the candlestick holder for fifty-odd quid; so that the said despicable Eric would get his money back and Cathy would get her perfect present.

Then, somewhat unusually for a man under pressure, Chris had a completely brilliant idea.

'A hundred and ten, eh? Let me just give it another quick once-over then.'

'Well…' Eric handed it over. 'Just be careful with it.'

'I will,' said Chris, hoping that a spot of drastic action would get the price down. 'Oops…'

The candlestick holder hit the ground and broke into four or five pieces.

'Oh my God,' gasped Eric. 'What have you done, you idiot!'

Just carrying out a brilliant plan, mate.

'You must let me give you your money back, Eric. Fifty-five quid, wasn't it?'

13. CATHY

It was Christmas Eve teatime, it was cold and Cathy was outside a bookshop in Leicester. It hadn't been difficult – simply a matter of checking the publisher's website for details of Jim Rae's only UK book-signing gig.

How she despised him.

Still, it had been a worthwhile visit to Leicester. She'd been able to see her main rival: King Richard the Third. Well, his tomb, at least. Ever since they had dug him up from a local pub car park and planted his bones in the cathedral, he'd been sucking tourist numbers out of Castle Hill. That was something she'd have to put right. But right now, she had another unhelpful famous figure in her sights.

Peering through the shop window, she had a clear view of her target.

Look at him, sitting there with no-one interested in his stupid book. Well, okay, six or seven people then.

At least the rain had stopped, although that had coaxed a guitar-jangling busker to come out and ruin

"Hey Jude", which was particularly infuriating as it lasted seven minutes.

It had been a difficult time. Chris's proclamation of prezzie-buying success had been underlined with a degree of smugness that suggested he'd got her a place on the judging panel at the World Chocolate Cake Championship. That had left Cathy to mull over the best way to get a fishing freak to forget that their paths had crossed.

She found herself humming.

Na-na-na-na, hey Jim.

What struck her most, standing in the cold in Leicester, was that letting a fish fiend outsmart an intelligent woman went against the laws of nature. So, with that in mind, she pulled on a blonde wig, wrapped a scarf across her mouth and prepared to speak in a fake American accent.

Here we go then…

Removing the book from the carrier bag, she took a fortifying breath and stepped inside to join the queue.

'I'm sorry, you can't bring your own book,' said a stern female shop assistant wearing unfriendly glasses.

Cathy went over to her. She didn't want Jim hearing.

'It's okay, I bought it here,' she said softly. 'I only just heard of the book-signing.'

'Do you have a receipt?'

'Yes.'

'May I see it?'

'See what?'

'The receipt?'

'Ah, you're probably not aware of the circumstances of me buying the book – when that bag-snatcher grabbed my bag and all I could hang on to was this. Happy Christmas, by the way. Oh, I do love bookshops at this time of year. How's business been?'

'Business has been fine – mainly because people generally buy books from us rather than turn up with their own.'

'My husband's the one who actually came in to buy it. Tall, friendly. Do you remember him?'

'No.'

'He's a huge fan of Jim's but he didn't know there would be a signing. I mean you can't ask him to pay twice. Not with his in-growing toenail. I mean he'd hobble down here himself but you'd have blood seeping out of his shoe onto the carpet and nobody wants that.'

The shop assistant sighed and got back to her cataloguing, while a relieved Cathy joined the queue, which had shrunk to three, including herself.

Then two.

For a moment, she wondered if she was in the right bookshop. The author was chatting away like a contender for World's Friendliest Man.

And then, as a grotty, smelly male turned away, it was her turn. All it required was a bit of calm and a good, strong American accent. No need to say much; just thrust the book in front of the little toad and get him to sign his name.

'Could you make it to Chris, please.'

'Chris… of course… no trouble whatsoever. Is that an American accent I detect?'

'Yes.'

'East Coast?'

'Yes.'

This was annoying. The twit was obviously under orders from his agent to engage with his public. She could see the fake bonhomie in his eyes.

'I've got family there,' he said. 'Which part are you from?'

'The least-known bit.'

'Oh… now you sound Irish. Moved around, eh?'

'Yes, we moved around when I was little.'

'Devon too?'

'Please sign the book. I'm late for a hospital meeting. If I don't get there, it'll be medical chaos.'

Jim Rae shrugged and signed the book "To Chris, Best wishes, Jim Rae" but he failed to hand it over.

'You look familiar.'

'No, I don't.'

'It's you, isn't it.'

'No, it's not me at all.'

'Yes it is – the mad woman.'

'Give me that.'

Cathy grabbed the book and pulled.

Jim Rae pulled back.

There was a tug of war across the table, then Jim overstretched and fell forward, scattering copies of his book across the floor. Cathy turned and ran, past the unhelpful shop assistant, past two fishing people coming in, *ha ha*, and… 'Oof!' into the busker, sending a guitar and a signed book skidding across

the pavement, through a puddle and into the road…
where a car swerved to avoid the musical instrument
but not *From Barbel to Zander: In Search of an Angling
Paradise* by Jim Rae.

14. CHRISTMAS DAY

Chris opened his eyes in semi-dark.

Christmas morning.

His body was warm and snug under the duvet. His head though was freezing. He glanced at the clock. 7:28. The central heating wouldn't be firing up for another thirty-two minutes.

He hadn't expected to wake up early on Christmas morning, but, for the first time in years, he was feeling a little bit of excitement. The obvious thing to do would be to go downstairs, turn the heating on manually, make some tea and bring the presents up. But that would mean getting out of bed.

Hmmm.

What if Cathy got up first, made some tea and brought the presents up?

He gave her a nudge.

'Happy Christmas, Cath.'

'Uhh uhmm mmm sss.'

'If only I could see your gorgeousness in this dim light.' He waited a moment. 'If only someone would get up and open the curtains.' He waited a moment longer. 'Someone who sleeps nearer the window than me.'

'Uhh mmm nrr.'

'And then, while they were up, they could nip downstairs and override the central heating timer switch. And possibly make a cup of tea.'

'Oggoff.'

Chris threw off the duvet causing a Big Draft. As he opened the curtains, a voice from under the other part of the duvet uttered, 'Tea, please.'

Chris harrumphed theatrically, donned his dressing gown and went downstairs.

In the kitchen, Truly-Trudy looked up from her basket, possibly wondering why the heating couldn't stay on all night.

Chris got the boiler going and put the kettle on. Then he nipped into the lounge, where he took the present Cathy had got him from under the tree.

'Good ol' Cath.'

He admired the neat wrapping with his name on. It looked great, it felt great, and it… smelled funny.

He sniffed closer.

'Interesting aroma…'

As he headed back to the kitchen, he wondered if they shouldn't have their tea downstairs. Seeing as he was already up. Maybe a bit of shouting up the stairs would do the trick.

Two minutes later, Cathy came down looking sleepy in her dressing gown.

'Tea? Bed?' she queried.

'I thought, as it's Christmas morning, we'd have

tea by the tree.'

He handed her a steaming mug.

'Well,' she croaked, sitting down on the sofa, 'I suppose it's a more romantic start to the day.'

'Exactly! And we have things to unwrap, Cath. Things that will reveal our souls to each other. At least I hope there's some soul in what you wrapped up because the body's definitely decomposing.'

'You don't get that with gift vouchers,' said Cathy, prior to sipping her tea.

Chris handed her the perfect gift.

Cathy put her mug down and frowned at the haphazard wrapping.

'Won't you ever learn how to use scissors and tape?'

But she relented. He meant well. He always meant well.

'You first,' she said.

'Right!'

Chris tore the wrapping off and let it fall to the floor. He was holding a book. A *fishing* book.

'It's the new one!' he exclaimed. He opened it. 'Wow, it's been signed by... Yin Run.'

'Jim Rae, you twit.'

'Just teasing. It's a brilliant present. Did you see him in Leicester?'

Cathy was amazed.

'How did you know I saw him in Leicester?'

'It said in *Fishing Monthly* he'd be there signing copies. I was thinking of popping over there myself and getting one but I'd spent all my money.'

Chris picked up the copy of *Fishing Monthly* that

had been open on the coffee table since Saturday morning and pointed to the little advert. Cathy felt the Christmas spirit beginning to leave her body. She had to reel it back in.

'You probably don't know this, Chris, but I don't always find time to read that most excellent of publications. I had to rely on a different method. You know the one; buying an unsigned copy and going round to the miserable old goat's house. Only, he threatened to call the police. Then I had to stalk him while he was fishing and, this time, he really did call the police, who happened to be sitting a few yards away with a rod. So, by the time I got around to the book shop in Leicester…'

'…you were like old friends! Ha-ha! Brilliant! Wait till I tell my old fishing mates in London. Cathy, you've made my Christmas. What a star you are!'

He leaned in and kissed her.

'I'm glad you're happy, Chris.'

'Happy? It's the perfect present! Even if it *is* a bit damp and going mouldy. Now, what about yours?'

'Okay, so what have we here…?'

'Before you open it, I just want you to know that it was no trouble at all to find you the perfect gift and to do battle at the auction. Chasing the bloke who bought it out of the auction and along the High Street was just part of the fun. And, as for having to pay the crook way over the odds, well, for you, my love, it was all worth it.'

Cathy unwrapped it carefully.

'Chris, it's damaged.'

'It was the only way I could get him to sell it to me at an affordable price. Still, you'll notice I've expertly repaired it. And I do mean expertly. After all, I have experience in repairing this particular style of candlestick holder.'

'It's…'

'It's one of a matching pair, yes. I mean they couldn't be more matched. Even the big gluey crack is in the same place. I blame the factory for using weak clay, myself. The Victorians obviously had their Friday afternoon manufacturing issues. Still, they're a fine pair and that's all that matters. I mean who cares that one is taller than the other with a slightly different pattern.'

'Yes, they're a funny pair,' said Cathy. 'Odd and cracked.'

'A bit like us,' said Chris.

Cathy couldn't stop herself laughing.

'Chris, it's the perfect gift.'

'Really?'

It wasn't really perfect, of course, but Chris's efforts more than made up for it. She was happy. The radiators were hot, the mince pies could be heated quite quickly and no couple could have tried harder to show their love through the age-old institution of gift-buying. And that included Jasmine arranging for Roland to be fitted for a Savile Row suit and Roland sorting out glider lessons for Jasmine. Sitting back on the sofa, Cathy rested her hands on her tummy. The perfect gift? Well, she would need a biological miracle to receive that.

Chris moved in close, causing a mini earthquake.

'Our first Christmas in Castle Hill,' he said.

He wrapped an arm around her and pulled her in tight. She melted into him.

'Are you happy to give it a go, Chris?'

'As long as it's me and you against the world, I'm happy to give anything a go, Cath. Except waxing. I'm not having my body hair ripped off for no-one.'

Cathy smiled. Chris really was a good man. He'd make a bloody good dad too. But now she was dreaming again. Although, it didn't hurt to dream, did it? After all, it was Christmas.

THE END

More books from the author…

CATHY & CHRIS
UNDER SIEGE
(full length novel)

*"Humorous, tongue-in-cheek, writing
that is very entertaining."*

U.S. reviewer

Cathy's new job at a Norman castle in Leicestershire
supports her joint passions: bringing history to the
people and proving her family's link to the founding
of the castle all those centuries ago.

Meanwhile, Chris is getting busy enjoying the local
inland waterways.

It really is perfect.

Until it all goes wrong.

OLIVIA HOLMES HAS INHERITED A VINEYARD

(full length novel)

*"It's increasingly rare to come across
a book brimming with such unashamed positivity.
I loved it."*

UK reviewer

In this Amazon UK bestseller, 44-year-old
Londoner Olivia Holmes has a demanding office
job, a big mortgage, and an underwhelming love life.

So, when she and two distant cousins inherit a
ramshackle vineyard, she just may have found a
wonderful distraction from her everyday existence.

However, there's a catch…

THOSE LAZY, HAZY, CRAZY DAYS OF SUMMER
(full length novel)

"I enjoyed the heck outta this story."

U.S. reviewer

As part of four generations, from baby to great-grandparents, Laura Cass – newly promoted to the role of grandma – is looking forward to the kind of seaside break her family has enjoyed seemingly forever.

However, this year, just when her wisdom and guidance is needed most, lonely Laura's desire to find out what happened to her 'first love' – a local boy – gets out of control…

THE GIRL WHO LIVED BY THE RIVER

(full length novel)

"Hugely enjoyable. This is a must for anyone who likes wry, comedic, coming of age stories."

UK reviewer

1975. Two teenagers. She plays cello. Will she teach him to play guitar?

This uplifting story is set in those far-off days of swapping LPs at school, searching for the inner poet, and practising guitar chords on a battered acoustic with three strings missing.

Against a backdrop of dock closures, the rise of the National Front, and the birth of punk rock, we follow would-be musical force Tom Alder's hilarious and ultimately touching rite of passage in late-1970s Britain.

Both heartfelt and honest, The Girl Who Lived by the River is an unforgettable celebration of the joys and agonies of growing up.

Printed in Great Britain
by Amazon

31529940R00058